The Girl
in the Golden Dress

Story: Jan Paul Schutten

Illustrations: Martijn van der Linden

Translation: Laura Watkinson

RUBINSTEIN

ISBN 9789047615248

First edition, 2013
© Rubinstein Publishing bv, Amsterdam
© Text: Jan Paul Schutten, 2012
© Illustrations: Martijn van der Linden, 2012
Translation: Laura Watkinson
Design: Ubald Seveke

This book was created in collaboration with Het Rijksmuseum, Amsterdam

RIJKS MUSEUM

This is Nettie. She's wearing her very best clothes. Nettie's mother has spent hours and hours combing her hair, and the lady next door has given her a beautiful golden crown to wear.

But why is she dressed up so finely?

Nettie's not the only one. She's surrounded by a group of guardsmen. They're dressed just as nicely as Nettie. And what a fuss they're making! They keep asking one another, "How does my collar look?", "What about my hair?" and "Is my hat on straight?"

There's so much hustle and bustle that it's hard to spot Nettie in the crowd.

But why are they all so excited?

That's because it's a very big day for the guards. Rembrandt, the best and most famous artist in the land, is going to paint them.

Nettie takes a look around. There are so many people.
Will they all fit in one painting? She'd really like to know.
So she goes over to Rembrandt and asks him.

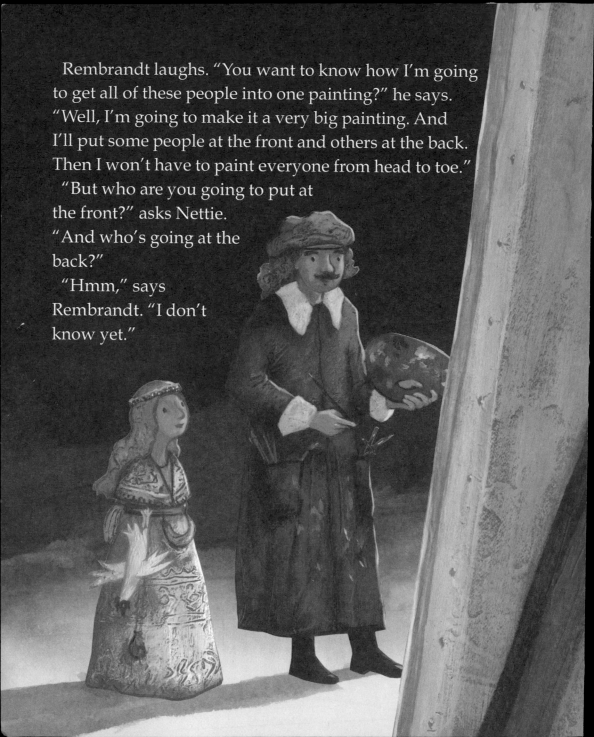

Rembrandt laughs. "You want to know how I'm going to get all of these people into one painting?" he says. "Well, I'm going to make it a very big painting. And I'll put some people at the front and others at the back. Then I won't have to paint everyone from head to toe."

"But who are you going to put at the front?" asks Nettie. "And who's going at the back?"

"Hmm," says Rembrandt. "I don't know yet."

"Perhaps I'll put the most important guard at the front…" says Rembrandt.

"The most important one?" cries the man with the red sash. "Then I should be at the front. I'm the most important one, because I am the captain of all the guards."

"If it weren't for me, this city would be full of rogues and villains," the man with the red sash continues. "I'm the one who orders my men to round up the criminals and put them in prison. So it's me who makes sure the city is a safe place to live."

"But perhaps I should put the bravest guard at the front," says Rembrandt to Nettie.

"The bravest one?" says the man in the golden clothes. "Then you should put me at the front. Because I'm the bravest guard. I once chased a criminal to the top of the Westerkerk tower. It was so high… And so scary… But I still did it. I caught him right at the very top and then I marched him off to prison."

"Or I could put the cleverest guard at the front," says Rembrandt.

"The cleverest one?" says the man in the tall hat. "That would be me, of course. I always come up with the best ideas even in the strangest situations."

"This one time, I'd cornered a gang of thieves," continues the man in the tall hat. "But I didn't have anything to tie them up with. And they outnumbered me. They could have attacked me at any moment, because the whole gang of them was so much stronger than just me on my own. I knew that if I didn't quickly come up with something clever, they would escape. Do you know what I did?"

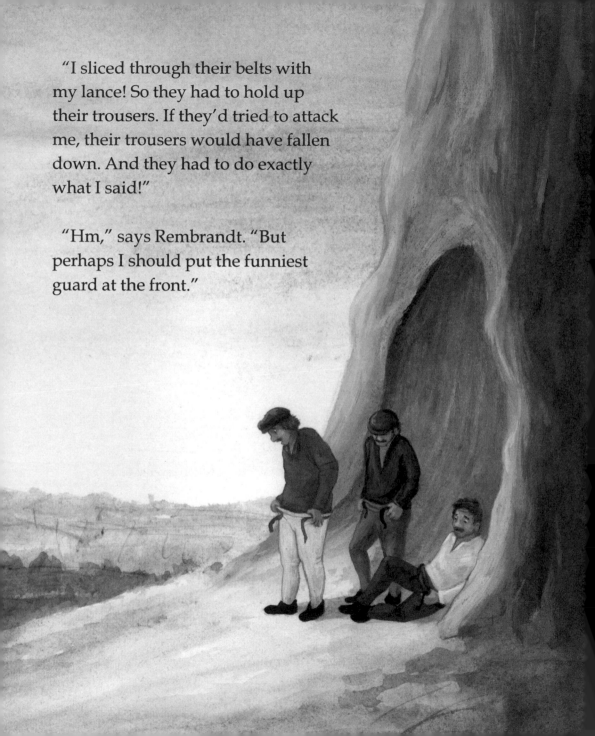

"I sliced through their belts with my lance! So they had to hold up their trousers. If they'd tried to attack me, their trousers would have fallen down. And they had to do exactly what I said!"

"Hm," says Rembrandt. "But perhaps I should put the funniest guard at the front."

"The funniest one?" says the man in the funny hat. "Then it's me you want! I once spotted a bunch of crooks, but I didn't have any weapons with me. I shouted at someone to go for help but, in the meantime, I had to make sure the crooks didn't get away. So what did I do? I told them lots of jokes. I made them laugh so hard that they were rolling on the ground."

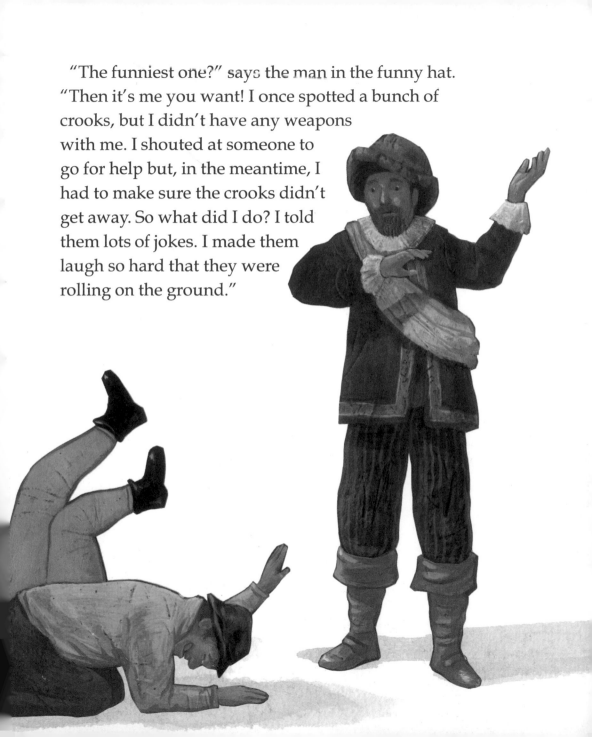

"And if you're lying on the ground, you can't
run away," continues the man in the funny hat.
"So I went on cracking jokes until the guards
came to arrest them and throw them into prison!"

"Or perhaps I should put the most charming person at the front," says Rembrandt.

Just then, a man arrives with a tray full of food and drinks.

"Mister Rembrandt, Miss Nettie. Would you like a little something to eat or drink? Don't the two of you look lovely! Your hair really suits you like that, Miss Nettie. And, Mister Rembrandt, you paint so beautifully."

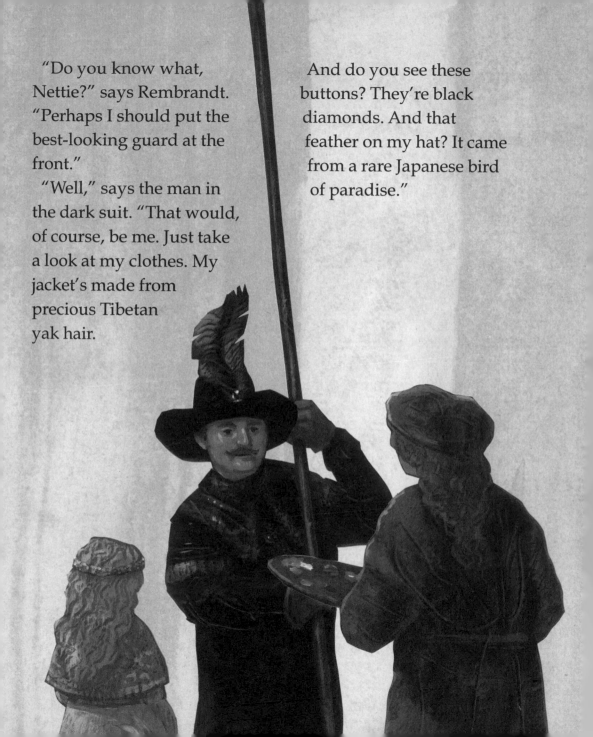

"Do you know what, Nettie?" says Rembrandt. "Perhaps I should put the best-looking guard at the front."

"Well," says the man in the dark suit. "That would, of course, be me. Just take a look at my clothes. My jacket's made from precious Tibetan yak hair.

And do you see these buttons? They're black diamonds. And that feather on my hat? It came from a rare Japanese bird of paradise."

"Oh dear," says Nettie. "I shouldn't be here at all. I'm not important, or brave, or clever, or funny, or charming, or good-looking. I don't belong in this painting. Not even right at the back."

"No, Nettie!" calls Rembrandt. "Don't go!"

But it's too late. Nettie's already gone.

Weeks go by. After a while, Nettie forgets all about the painting.

But one day the captain of the guards comes to see her. "Nettie!" he calls. "Come on! Rembrandt's finished. He's going to show us the painting."

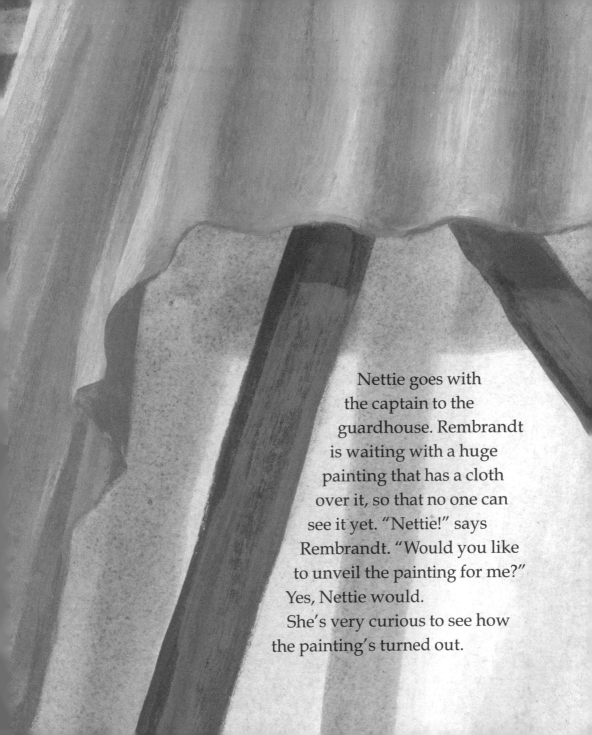

Nettie goes with
the captain to the
guardhouse. Rembrandt
is waiting with a huge
painting that has a cloth
over it, so that no one can
see it yet. "Nettie!" says
Rembrandt. "Would you like
to unveil the painting for me?"
Yes, Nettie would.
She's very curious to see how
the painting's turned out.

"I'm right at the front!" cries Nettie. "And I'm standing in the light, too!"

Rembrandt laughs. "I wasn't sure whether to put the bravest, the cleverest or the most important one at the front..." he says. "But I was certain that the sweetest person in the room should have pride of place!"